Published in the United States by Ragged Bears, Inc.
413 Sixth Avenue, Brooklyn, New York 11215

www.raggedbears.com

Originally published in Great Britain in 1998 by Ragged Bears Publishing
Milborne Wick, Sherborne, Dorset DT9 4PW

CIP Data is available

First American edition. Printed and bound in China.

ISBN 1-929927-12-6

2 4 6 8 10 9 7 5 3 1

Ragged Bears

Brooklyn, New York • Milborne Wick, Dorset

Little Mouse

HAS A FRIEND

Steve Lavis

Today Little Mouse and his friend are going to the beach.

They jump in the car and drive off. Soon they see the ocean.

Together, they splash in the waves.

Then they play soccer.
Little Mouse is the goalie.

Their picnic lunch is delicious.

The two friends hunt for shells.

They use the shells to
decorate their
sandcastle.

The sun is setting, so they head for home. This has been a perfect day to share with a friend.